EASTER
COLORING BOOK

THIS BOOK BELONGS TO

· ·

EASTER COLORING BOOK

EASTER COLORING BOOK

EASTER COLORING BOOK

EASTER COLORING BOOK

EASTER COLORING BOOK

EASTER COLORING BOOK

EASTER COLORING BOOK

EASTER COLORING BOOK

EASTER COLORING BOOK

EASTER COLORING BOOK